DARPA

THE RISE

Vol. V

MANUEL PELAEZ

DARPA
THE RISE

MANUEL PELAEZ

Darpa the Rise by Manuel Pelaez

ISBN 978-1-970072-12-9 (Paperback)
ISBN 978-1-970072-15-0 (Hardback)

Printed in the United States of America.

New Leaf Media, LLC
175 S. 3rd Street, Suite 200
Columbus, OH 43215
www.thenewleafmedia.com

INTRODUCTION

T he entire DARPA series, is like the birth of a living star, where the concentration of energies from within gives so much life to everything in its reach. Supplying all the elements to inspire others to unleash all their full potentials across the universe, Manuel Pelaez.

CHAPTER 1

The rise of the world's greatest nightmare has risen, the greatest modern prophecy has been fulfilled. Let us all pray for this nightmare to have mercy upon the world, in every corner of our world everyone from children to elders shall hear the term (THE NEW ORDER). Somewhere in the Islamic world and under a shield of heavy state of the art sophisticated anti-missile systems. Using modern electronic warfare (EW) jammers, and other state of the art devices. A heavy presence of guards with modern warfare weapons, security is imperative. The messiah will speak in front of thousands and thousands of people waiting to get a glimpse of him. The crowds are extremely eager to hear every drop of sacred words which is written in prophecy. This moment is the enlightenment of his children all gathered patiently. The following are ground shaking speeches that will embrace the spirit, freedom, rejuvenation of the soul. It's thunder flowing through your body, a transformation of the mind and spirit, cleansing your very existence. It is an awakening, listening to the messiah it gives anyone goosebumps all over your inner being. Everything the messiah says is so true it's absolutely rejuvenating. It's like shedding your old soul and embracing a new reinforced one. One can feel that energy everywhere, it's an incredible opportunity to be in this divine presence. The following are a series of speeches from the messiah himself speaking in front of thousands and thousands of people.

Chapter 2

Speaking in Russian-Arabic language, let's begin, I stand here today, to inhale all the suffering of the world. I can feel their pain throughout my body that serves as a vessel between two worlds. I stand here today, to absorb all this pain from the core of its surroundings. I will eliminate these emotions physically, mentally, and spiritually. I stand here today, for my children to witness the eradication of human ideologies. Lift your arms up high, to be freed from these damnations. I leave my old soul behind and embrace the greater spirit. Cleansing my body and soul to become a renewed existence.

Chapter 3

Standing in front of the crowds there was a very special woman called (Cyra), which means in Persian, "Sun, throne, or lord". These speeches were done throughout a period of months, let's continue to the next speech.

Chapter 4

I stand here today, witnessing the absolute destruction that the modern world has posed upon our beautiful world. We look at how our oceans have deteriorated. We see how we have lost habitable lands; we see the very air we breathe poisoned. I stand here today, embracing the pain of so many innocent civilizations. The poison that is caused by the modern world will be irreversible if not stopped. The human race must do better and not bow down to financial interests and corporations. I stand here today, teaching my children the ancient scriptures to free themselves.

Chapter 5

With every speech (Cyra) grew more closer to the messiah and her passion was noticed. Let's move on to the next speech, I stand here today, inhaling all the souls that have fought in so many wars throughout history. These brave spirits stand with me together even when they all died by the hands of human ideologies.Look closely my children and you can see millions of brave souls standing with me. I have set them all free from humanity to embrace their rightful place as brothers and sisters not enemies.I stand here today, to free all the souls that can see pass their flesh selves and are limited. Free yourselves and embrace your rightful place beyond anything humanity has to offer you. Now, we continue to the final speech prepare yourselves, let's begin.

Chapter 6

I stand here today, to inhale all the abusive propaganda and brainwashing from the modern world. Look closely at how each of you are living, controlled and overtaken by technologies. Your very souls are poisoned, your thoughts are manipulated.I stand here today, to show my children that the modern world feeds you poison. Look at the foods you eat, everything is subsidized by chemicals. Look at what your lives have become, your sheep or robots being told what to do on a daily basis. I stand here today, for all the poor souls that can't take it anymore. Being abused in a financial network that keeps you suffocated and tormented. I stand here today, to show my children that the ancient ways are better, more fulfilling, better overall for your souls. Adaptations in weaponry and medicine are embraced, simply because the modern world will never stop their dominant ways. Science can be used only in areas of necessity for better health and prevent any attacks to our sacred lifestyles. Stand with me my children and rebuke the modern world with all its poison. May, my words reach your souls like the air that flows everywhere, freeing each of you from your damnations.

CHAPTER 7

After each of the ground shaking speeches, everybody in attendance gets up and starts clapping, the overwhelming cheers and emotions. The crowds roar echoes throughout. The messiah sends some of his loyalists to invite Cyra to be with him, finally the messiah seems to have met someone special. Cyra, accepts the invitation and she is eager to meet with the messiah, this relationship will have a significant meaning later on. Both the messiah and Cyra, exchange in conversation talking about each other, she is delighted to be in the presence of the messiah. If you're wondering, since the beginning of the speeches and as Cyra was being noticed, the messiah had Cyra cleared by his loyalists and spiritual advisors. Absolutely no one can get close to the messiah without being cleared, even Cyra knows how important the messiah is and what is his promise to fulfill prophecy. Their love for each other grew into something pretty spectacular, for the first time the messiah was happy after suffering such overwhelming losses. This love for each other was honored by everyone and they both had an ancient traditional marriage.

CHAPTER 8

The day Cyra told the messiah that she was pregnant, the news spread and the spiritual visions saw a baby girl. The name of this baby girl is also extremely important, she shall bear the name (Siria) which means in Persian "sun-bright or glowing". This name has significant meaning and purpose later on as things progress, a lot of turmoil is coming soon as the story is revealed.

Chapter 9

In the meantime, during the very beginning when the speeches first started, somewhere in space. DARPA's satellites which are part of their space force happens to capture the speeches from the messiah.Even though, the speeches are somewhere in the Middle East and they do have state of the art anti-missile systems, drones, and modern jet fighters. The technologies that DARPA has in space are capable of picking up conversations on the earth's surface. Worldwide, the nuclear capabilities were disabled by the Massive Space Energy Sphere after they left the earth's atmosphere. Now, all types of conflicts will strictly be conventional warfare, humanity cannot be trusted with such destructive nuclear weapons.

Chapter 10

A meeting at DARPA's headquarters is about to take place regarding the speeches of the messiah and how to take protective measures in their security apparatus worldwide. Even though, the speeches were made in Russian-Arabic, it is translated into many languages to review the content by neighboring partners of DARPA. Inside the conference room of DARPA, Director Jones, military personnel, the team of robotic engineering scientists, and other experts. Keep in mind, Whit and Shu are busy coordinating with other special ones and cadets the reopening of (UNI-WORLD) in many locations worldwide. The meeting begins, let's play each of the speeches sentence by sentence, breaking them down to see if there are encrypted messages hidden. We need to monitor these developments closely, increasing are alert levels, reinforce security. We cannot underestimate Ron Ben Ruckman, we must remember he is a brilliant scientist take has been completely transformed into a messiah. After everyone listened to the speeches they were deeply disturbed, the fury and hatred towards the modern world was unbelievable. His fellow colleagues were saddened by what he has become, it is crystal clear that the ex-scientist poses a real threat to DARPA and the modern world. His fellow colleagues were deeply shocked that the ex-scientist is the same person they knew. The ex-scientist has been radicalized by extremists beyond any type of reason, little did everyone inside DARPA's conference room realize the extent of events about to take place in the near future. The conclusion, of the meeting clearly see's that the ex-scientist Ron Ben Ruckman hatred towards modern science was the pursuit of leaders achieving ultimate destructive weapons like (zero-point energy and nuclear technologies), which led to great loss of deaths.

CHAPTER 11

Meanwhile, back at the unknown location in the Middle East where the messiah is located. The messiah is present to see the birth of his only daughter (Siria), it brings joy to him after she is born to hold such a beautiful baby girl in his arms. Siria, will become the heir to the messiah's prophecy and will be under protective guard to ensure her safety. Siria, when she is old enough will be taught everything about science to become a great scientific mind as her father the messiah. Now, it's time for the messiah to fulfill prophecy and create the deadliest unknown weapons to bring down DARPA. The messiah has a secret chamber with a team of other scientists to begin the tasks at hand. This secret chamber has sound proof walls and a lead base exterior to prevent any electronic devices from recording or detection. A significant amount of time will pass by until these lethal weapons are created. In the meantime, Siria will continue growing up until she will begin learning about science. Before the team starts, the messiah gives a small speech inside the chamber to the team about the tasks ahead. Phase one, is to develop microscopic Nanobots inside tiny flash drives USB memory sticks, these are tiny in nature but have the ability to store a massive amount of information.

CHAPTER 12

For starters, the speeches are all available to listen to, this is solely for the purpose of recruiting. Turning many into sympathizers of their cause, by listening to the intoxicating speeches their minds and spirits are freed. Phase two, is even more complicated, inside the tiny flash drives are microscopic Nanobots with deadly viruses. War against invisible weapons, unofficial-official cyber warfare, in which lines of code are the new Kalashnikovs, holding enough power to cripple infrastructure, and even kill. From the birth of deadly viruses such as worms, trojans, and virus's evolution. Ryuk, Cyborg, Cryptomix Clop, BorOntOK, Yatron, Astaroth, Go Brut, Jokeroo, Gandcrab, Trojan Glupteba, Kuik Adware, Magniber, Thanatos, trojan Panda Banker/Zeus Panda. Even more advanced viruses, Moker remote access Trojan, Stuxnet, Mydoom, Sobig, Klez, ILoveYou, Wanna Cry, Zues, Code Red, Slammer, CryptoLocker, Sasser. We will create Nanobots, microscopic an armada of small robots. Phase three, we will also create protective suits that shied us from attacks against our Nanobots. DARPA, does have sophisticated cyber security and antivirus systems, but what we are creating is a first in futuristic technologies never seen before. Phrase four, is to launch these Nanobots into DARPA's technologies causing significant damage, disabling their systems. Windows of opportunities will be developed when the sympathizers embrace our cause. The messiah and the rest of the scientists get busy to work, conducting experiments. The scientific experiments are tested carefully, the messiah leads with overall knowledge and precision. A significant of time passes by and Siria his daughter is growing up like any normal kid.

CHAPTER 13

As time goes by life in the modern world goes on with all the agreements formed during the DARPA conferences. Whit and Shu have taught the other special ones that have abilities like them to communicate with the land and sea creatures of our world. There's plenty of cadets also helping out, (UNI-WORLD) habitats are reopened around the world. The agreements during the DARPA conferences are being implemented, vital issues like the earth's food supply for the future. The earth's human growth populations, and construction is ongoing for solar power stations in space. Photovoltaic Array converts the sunlight into electricity, electromagnetic radiation non-ionizing radiation frequencies. Earth finally seems to be on track for a brighter future with the assistance of DARPA and other nations worldwide. Laws are in place to protect the land and sea creatures from becoming extinct. Fines and punishments are written and enforced; the human race seems to be learning how vital our world truly is. Unlike a dream come true not everyone seems to honor these dramatic changes. For instance, making hunting and fishing illegal, and banning recreational boating. These laws did not resonate with many people worldwide, sacrifices are crucial to secure a future for animals and sea creatures from extinction. The challenges are overwhelming for DARPA and other nations to enforce, using advanced technologies also spies on people constantly. These technologies are the future and their capabilities are impressive, patrolling the world's oceans and lands. Cargo ship vessels transport, semi-trucks transport, plastic products, rubber, and trash. Worldwide measures are reshaping our world to avoid disasters not contaminate our environments. The DARPA conferences addressed all the major world issues and energy resources for futures to come. DARPA's new headquarters in located in a unknown location in the great state of Texas. DARPA's new headquarters is heavily fortified by advanced technologies such as autonomous supersonic jet fighter drones, autonomous robotic super solders, (HEL) high energy laser towers. All DARPA compounds have the same technologies and securities, which makes things extremely difficult for any foe to trespass or cause any damage. DARPA even patrols the coastlines and oceans with autonomous weaponized underwater drones. Any major conflict and the United States armed forces are on standby to assist whenever necessary.

Chapter 14

Back at the messiah location, the Nanobots are created in the laboratories inside the protective chambers. Now, the laboratories shall manufacture a mass production of tiny flash drives that can be plugged into any electronic devices. Inside each tiny flash drive shall have the microscopic Nanobots and intoxicating speeches, which are both meant to infest the electrical systems of DARPA and turn many into sympathizers for their cause. A movement shall be formed called (Liberation) among those who are against the modern world with all its restrictions and laws. The master plan is to send teams of infiltrators to penetrate these groups and supply them with the tiny flash drives. The point of entry into DARPA's systems are the cadets, all it takes is for one cadet to plug into DARPA's systems with any electronic devices which includes, television, monitor, radio, computers. The targets are DARPA compounds, which are at different locations worldwide, (UNI-WORLD) will be the easiest way to penetrate their systems. The Nanobots are smart microscopic self-learning robots, meaning they have the capabilities of entering any electrical currents as long as it's in the same region. These means if a (UNI-WORLD) is located near a DARPA compound the Nanobots can move within their electrical systems. What the Nanobots can't do is cross oceans to other regions, this technology is a first of its kind and can penetrate DARPA's sophisticated cyber security and antivirus protections.

CHAPTER 15

S iria, the messiah's daughter timeline, she is already eight years old and striving in basic science. Siria, understands her crucial role and has everything from private teachers and monitors 24/7. She's beginning to understand her importance since being the only heir to the messiah's prophecy, one day she will carry on that prophecy fulfillment.

CHAPTER 16

After more time passes by the mass production of tiny flash drives are complete. Teams of infiltrators are sent to different locations around the world, where they will join the protestors that are against DARPA and the modern world changes. Canada, Siberia, Alaska, Africa, Madagascar, Australia, and Costa Rica, are the locations of the different habitats of (UNI-WORLD). The secret DARPA compounds are located in unknown locations in the deserts of Nevada and Texas. It is not known exactly where the others are like in Canada and Siberia which are foreign countries. Accumulating where the DARPA compounds are located is key to proceed forward. The infiltrators will be at these locations patiently waiting to join the protestors and somehow recruit cadets that can enter the DARPA compounds by request only. The plan goes into effect and the infiltrators living quarters are in key locations. As time passes by the infiltrators are successful in joining the protestors which using have peaceful demonstrations near (UNI-WORLD) and other locations. The infiltrators begin the movement (Liberation), it inspires many protesters, some are ready for the next phase. When protesters show they truly hate DARPA and the modern world changes, they earn a tiny flash drive to begin hearing the intoxicating speeches. Some of the protesters know some of the cadets that aren't so loyal to DARPA and the modern world changes. This plan is taking place in the other countries also, for instance, the (UNI-WORLD) in Siberia is controlled by the Russian military advanced technologies, their version of DARPA. The other countries where the (UNI-WORLD) habitats are located its the United States in coordination with ally countries. The protest that go on are individuals who are fed up with so many restrictions and laws, and advanced technologies taking over everything. Not everyone sees these changes as saving our world and the future of the human race. The protesters are organized and they carry signs, DARPA doesn't interfere with peaceful protests. Many protesters have embraced the movement (Liberation) and have influenced some cadets to join. The infiltrators know they cannot rush anything, they allow things to happen naturally without raising so much suspicion. Everything is unfolding naturally and more tiny flash drives are given out, the intoxicating speeches within the tiny flash drives seem to fill the void the protesters needed. Many protesters are ready for the next phase, this entire process took about two years to develop.

CHAPTER 17

At this time Siria, the daughter of the messiah is already eleven years old and striving with her basic science knowledge. Meanwhile, the protesters are intoxicated by the speeches and some of the cadets are willing to take the necessary risks to enter the DARPA compounds. The plan is for the protesters to cause distractions by starting fires and throwing things, breaking windows, etc. While some cadets leave (UNI-WORLD) asking for permission to talk to command at DARPA compounds to address their concerns about their safety and (UNI-WORLD). Hopefully, this will grant some of them entry into the DARPA compounds, to quickly plug in the tiny flash drives to any electronic devices. On a day where the weather was beautiful and everything was peaceful the plan goes into effect.

CHAPTER 18

First, it was the distractions of the protesters, setting things on fire, breaking windows, fighting. Immediately, this was detected by the autonomous supersonic jet-fighter drones and several autonomous super soldiers showed up. Some of the cadets request permission to talk to command in person to address their urgent concerns. Their request were granted and autonomous vehicles came to pick them up which were already inside (UNI-WORLD). To make things clear most of the cadets that work inside (UNI-WORLD) are extremely loyal and believe in DARPA and the modern world changes. In the DARPA compound in an unknown location in the desert of Nevada permission was granted instead of an autonomous vehicle, an autonomous supersonic jet-fighter drone is sent to pick some cadets up rather than taking days driving from Alaska to Nevada. In Texas, the compound of DARPA's new headquarters no access is granted to anyone because its classified. In Canada, permission is granted to some of the cadets, in Siberia, no access is granted to anyone because its classified. In Africa, access is granted to some of the cadets, in Madagascar, access is granted to some cadets. In Costa Rica, access is granted to some of the cadets, in Australia, no access is granted to anyone because its classified. The cadets have a small window of time in accordance to different regional time zones. This window of time has been calculated very carefully, broken up in travel time and opportunities.

Chapter 19

The following are the actual events in military time, travel time by air and land, broken up in sequences. In Alaska (UNI-WORLD) the protesters start rioting at 02:00 hours, some cadets call the DARPA compound in Nevada. Immediately, autonomous supersonic jet-fighter is on route upon request from (UNI-WORLD) to Nevada, flight time 5 hours. At (UNI-WORLD) outside perimeters, autonomous super-soldiers and personal are mobilized to encounter protesters. Deadly fire won't be used, only if necessary, tear gas and other chemicals are disbursed to dispense the crowds of protesters. At approximately, 07:00 hours autonomous supersonic jet-fighter with some cadet's land inside DARPA's compound in the unknown location in Nevada. The protesters in Canada start rioting at 09:00 hours outside (UNI-WORLD) perimeters, some cadets call the DARPA compound in an unknown location in Canada. Autonomous super-soldiers and personnel are mobilized to encounter and dispense the protesters. By 10:00 hours some cadets are already inside the DARPA compound in Canada. Across the world, in Africa the protesters start rioting at 04:00 hours outside (UNI-WORLD) perimeters. Some cadets call DARPA's compound from (UNI-WORLD) in Africa, supersonic jet-fighter is on route upon request. Super-soldiers and personal are mobilized to encounter and dispense the protesters. At approximately, the supersonic jet-fighter picks up and lands inside DARPA's compound in a unknown location in Africa at 05:00 hours. Systematically and synchronized, as the cadets are waiting in the lobby to speak to command, they see monitors mounted on the walls. Everyone is being constantly monitored inside the compound at all times.

CHAPTER 20

In minutes, each of the cadets plugged in the tiny flash drives to the backside of the monitor. The minute this happens emergency sirens sound everywhere, and immediately everything is shutdown. DARPA's emergency response systems quickly shutdown all energies to prevent major system damages. This includes the autonomous super-soldiers and autonomous supersonic jet-fighters, even the (HEL) high energy towers. The cadets attempted to run away in the cover of dark trying their best to leave the compound. Running for their lives to escape they are all met with a barrage of gunfire, some cadets are killed instantly. The others are wounded but captured, the personnel extract all personal items including the tiny flash drives. Instantly, when the emergency response systems were activated, the armed forces are mobilized to assist and secure the DARPA compounds. DARPA, is the pride of nations where the most advanced technologies are designed and executed.

Chapter 21

Meanwhile, before these events were taking place, the infiltrators all leave the countries their mission was based. Their missions were extremely successful but it took significant amounts of life. In Texas, the main headquarters of DARPA, when word of what happened reached Director Jones. He absolutely was infuriated and quickly assembled the team of robotic engineers to get to the bottom of these catastrophic events. The wounded cadets which are few were taken to military hospitals under strict guard. The contents of the tiny flash drives were flown immediately by military aircrafts to Texas for scientific overviews. The full assessment of damages are being processed 24/7 by teams of the armed forces and DARPA personnel. At the military hospitals the cadets are given very potent experimental drugs to confess about everything they know. This will last for weeks until they are so mentally induced and under the influence to be interrogated.

<h1 style="text-align:center">CHAPTER 22</h1>

Under the domestic terrorist's act, the cadets and any other perpetrators all rights are discarded. When this horrific news reached Whit and Shu, they were absolutely shocked that some of the cadets actually became sympathizers against DARPA. Director Jones, gives the order saying "I want full damage assessment reports of each DARPA compound, a complete list". "I want a full investigation on what happened and how everything developed". "I want a full scientific investigation on what caused these horrific events". "I want prosecution of those responsible without any delays". "I want new preventive measures to prevent these events from ever happening again". As the Director of the CIA, his words have a lot of weight and everyone jumps into action. While all this is taking place, the military secures each DARPA compound with brigade of soldiers heavily armed. Taking position on the outer perimeters of each DARPA compound, this agreement is a mutual response in case of emergencies.

CHAPTER 23

Quickly, the team robotic engineering scientists get to work in their classified laboratory, composed by Sam Andre Dame, Jon Tan Lan, and other experts all following the team leader Tim Von Gleason. Director John tells Tim Von Gleason, "I don't care who or how long it takes, get to the bottom of this before more attacks occur". The team of robotic engineering scientists are the top of their class and will work 24/7 to find answers. Investigations into what exactly happened continue from multiple agencies (FBI) Federal Bureau of Investigation, (CIA) Central Intelligence Agency, DARPA personnel and other agencies. Assessment damage reports are coming in from Nevada in the United States. It is estimated that one quarter of the autonomous supersonic jet-fighters are completely lost. It is estimated that more than one quarter of the autonomous super-soldiers are gone. It is estimated that one quarter of the computer networks are lost, total amount of financial lost is estimated in 200 million dollars USD. Assessment damage reports are coming in from Canada, it is estimated that more than one quarter of the autonomous supersonic jet-fighters are gone. It is estimated that more than one quarter of the autonomous super-soldiers are damaged. It is estimated that more than one quarter of the computer networks are lost, total amount of financial lost is estimated in 300 million dollars USD. Assessment damage reports are coming in from Africa, it is estimated that more than one quarter of the autonomous supersonic jet-fighters are lost. It is estimated that more than one quarter of the autonomous super-soldiers were damaged. It is estimated that more than one quarter of the computer networks were damaged. The total amount of financial lost is estimated in 350 million dollars USD. The total financial lost in damages is staggering 850 million dollars USD, that's not even the worst part. It will take a significant amount of time in diagnostic evaluations, cleaning the internal systems, specialized parts, before all systems can function again properly. When the assessment damage reports came to the attention of Director Jones, after he carefully reviewed all the data. He was infuriated, by the amount of financial lose these events has inflicted on DARPA. Director Jones, actually shouted out "how in the hell did this happen", he quickly wanted answers.

Chapter 24

The investigations creating a timeline was already on the way, a team of agents from the (FBI) Federal Bureau of Investigation, (CIA) Central Intelligence Agency, DARPA personnel, and other agencies involved conclude an important meeting with Director Jones. The meeting takes place soon after all the pieces are put together, let's begin, teams of infiltrators arrive to targeted locations. Infiltrators carefully and methodically join the protesters, penetrating their groups with equal beliefs. The vulnerabilities of these groups through hatred and disbelief of DARPA and the modern world changes throughout our world. These infiltrators took years to select within the group's leaders that can be induced to other levels. The group leaders were given tiny flash drives which contain intoxicating speeches to fuel more hatred towards DARPA and the modern world changes. After these group leaders inspired more group members within the organized protesters. Some of these group members know some of the cadets, and slowly influenced them to join their cause. Slowly and methodically some of the cadets were induced into their cause and hatred towards DARPA and the modern world changes. The plan that took place was orchestrated and well organized, the cadets involved were gambling with the notion that if their lives were in jeopardy and they have major concerns on the safety of everyone inside (UNI-WORLD). DARPA command will not deny them a change to speak out, they actually requested permission to make everything seem normal. The cadets gamble became true and autonomous supersonic jet fighters were flown to pick them up and bring them to the DARPA compounds. The protesters rioting were just diversions to make things appear that (UNI-WORLD) was under siege and threatened. The acts of the cadets were systematically well planned out, synchronized to a timeline to plug in the tiny flash drives around the same time frame. The minute DARPA's emergency response was activated it shut down the entire compound avoiding further damages. At this time, the cadets attempted to escape under the cover of darkness, DARPA's personal are well armed and have thermal imaging technologies. DARPA personal are not visible around the compound, their post is hidden, due to the nature of DARPA's classified status. All this information was extracted by the wounded cadets inside military hospitals, under heavy sedated experimental drugs. These experimental drugs are given by military doctors and are highly effective, these perpetrators don't have any rights. At this time, the investigations conclude that the infiltrators all left the countries simultaneously after their missions are complete. What we know, the infiltrators all went to the Middle East before vanishing to an unknown location. The meeting comes to an end, now, Director Jones will gather more intel by meeting with the team of robotic engineering scientists. Perhaps, the science behind the tiny flash drives can reveal the answers we desperately need.

Chapter 25

After a short time, the next meeting between Director Jones and the team of robotic engineering scientists takes place. Tim Von Gleason, the leader of the team addresses Director Jones, by saying, "on behalf of myself and the rest of the team, we have good and bad news". Director Jones replies, "let's start with the bad news to get it out of the way first". Tim Von Gleason, and the rest of the team explain everything to Director Jones, let's begin, it will take years to crack the genetic code of the Nanobots. First of all, this is a revolutionary breakthrough in science, these Nanobots are microscopic in size. Self-learning smart intelligence, meaning the Nanobots can travel inside electrical currents. Not only can they bypass any cyber security or antivirus systems, but are capable of carrying the most innovative deadly viruses. Tim Von Gleason goes on to say "it's extraordinary science, we also examined the recordings". The recordings themselves are made up of brainwashing propaganda, extremely intoxicating when heard. The recordings induce a movement against DARPA and the modern world, we can easily notice how the infiltrators recruited others that were already displeased. The robotic engineering scientists conclude their findings to whom is behind these events. Without a doubt, between the science and the recordings, are conclusions are that Ron Ben Ruckman are former colleague is the main person behind these events. Director Jones says, "I can't believe it, someone that was a part of our team for many years". As the meeting went on, it seems that after Ron Ben Ruckman lost his pregnant wife and unborn baby, it was too much for him to bear. Once he fails under the radical extremists his hatred grew and grew, psychologically, mentally and spiritually, he has become someone else. Tim Von Gleason goes on to say, "we have detected a invisible signature blueprint in which the Nanobots leave a trace". He continues explaining, "scientifically speaking, in order to mass produce so many tiny flash drives, they were able to do so in some kind of plant, or a dedicated area". The team explains, "we ourselves had to create protective suits just to handle these Nanobots in a special laboratory". The team continues saying, "Without question, the scientists that created these Nanobots had to do the same thing". Director Jones says, " is there any way of knowing where their location is at exactly". The team respond by saying, "we can be certain that from our satellites in space they can pinpoint their location with this invisible signature blueprint created by the Nanobots". Director Jones says, " that's all I needed to hear, now, the next meeting will consist of moving forward, a strategic plan for an offensive attack". The team tells him, "he was our colleague and good friend", Director Jones goes on to say, " he was my friend also, but now Ron Ben Ruckman, has become an international most wanted terrorist, he is too far gone".

Chapter 26

The meeting has come to an end, meanwhile, Director Jones has received reports from the justice department that the perpetrators will receive a life sentence at a maximum-security prison. The corroborators of exciting riots during the protest to create diversions, will receive less punishable sentences. It is hard to pinpoint those corroborators, it is believed that not everyone knew about these coherent attacks. All the perpetrators including in Canada and Africa, will be sentenced to life at a maximum-security prison. Agreements are made in all countries where DARPA compounds are located, under the domestic terrorist's act. Two very important meetings are coming up, the first one is DARPA high command from the United States, Canada, and Africa, to introduce strict new measures on how to prevent these domestic terrorist's acts from ever happening again. The second meeting, will consist of how to design a strategic stealth offensive attack. Whit and Shu have requested to attend this important meeting due to their abilities if necessary, to launch forward such an attack. Director Jones, team of engineering scientists, military strategists, DARPA space force, Whit and Shu, will all be in attendance.

Chapter 27

irector Jones, doesn't waste any time, he takes off inside a military aircraft and heads out to Nevada first. Somewhere in the desert in an unknown location he lands inside the DARPA compound. Inside a top-secret conference room, he gathers with DARPA command and military personnel, after hours pass by. They all agree on the new measures to implement on all DARPA compounds, ensuring that these acts of domestic terrorism will never occur again. It is agreed that at no time any cadets cannot be given permission to enter any DARPA compound. All DARPA compounds will be classified top secret facilities, all cadets and DARPA personnel will undergo strict background checks. Some areas inside (UNI-WORLD) will be off limits, especially, where sensitive computer networks are located. The only classified permission will be granted to Whit and Shu, which are the heart and soul of our success worldwide. Everyone is in agreement with implementing these new preventive measures. Director Jones, can noticeably see how the DARPA compound functions are completely turned off and it will take some time to be cleared for normal operations again. Now, Director Jones, will take off to the DARPA compound in a unknown location in Canada. He brings with him, the new agreements to DARPA command there and see if they agree with these new security measures. Shortly afterwards, he lands inside the DARPA compound in Canada, he goes straight to a top-secret conference room and gathers with DARPA command. The leaders at DARPA command review the new security measures and are overall satisfied with how they pinpoint their concerns. The new security measures will go into effect immediately, now, Director Jones will take off to Africa which will be the last meeting. The military aircraft takes off from Canada to Africa, DARPA command there is on standby. Due to sensitive top-secret materials it is imperative to have these classified meetings in person. Flight time takes many hours but in a military supersonic jet fighter that time is shortened. Many hours later Director Jones arrives in Africa, he is accumulated in his quest quarters and prepares himself for the meeting with DARPA command. After being rested, Director Jones gathers with DARPA command, they review all the new measures and our very pleased with pinpointing exactly areas of concerns. Director Jones, can also visibly see how all the DARPA functions are turned off and military troops post outside protecting the compound. He tells DARPA command, "be patient, soon we will be fully functional again". He does not mention anything about the upcoming top secret classified meeting, because, the sensitive nature and timing it's developing. After the meeting and saying his goodbyes, Director Jones takes off to Texas, where the main headquarters of DARPA is located. After many hours, he lands inside DARPA main headquarters in Texas, somewhere in an unknown location in the desert.

Chapter 28

Now, Director Jones will be having the final meeting with many important guests to talk about an offensive attack. The highest-level classified meeting is now set, this meeting will include, Director Jones, DARPA space force, military strategists, team of robotic engineering scientists, Whit and Shu, and other experts. This meeting shall begin, first DARPA force will give their assessments, we have positioned our satellites in space to identify the invisible signature blueprints of the Nanobots on the earth's surface in the area where the infiltrators last fled and identified. We have pinpointed that location, the invisible signature blueprints from the Nanobots are extremely precise and no other substance can give these residues. Military strategists give their assessments, it is believed that in this location the Islamic State radicalized extremists has obtained either the S-400 or more advanced S-500 anti-ballistic missile systems. These missile systems also known as 55R6M "Triumfator", must have cost a fortune, and even worse. It makes even are supersonic stealth jet fighters obsolete against launching an attack even at supersonic speeds. The accuracy of these missile systems are extremely accurate and will spark an international incident that will lead to a major war. Whit, has an idea that is full proof and avoid such an incident from occurring, Whit goes on to say" this plan is carefully thought out. "The plan is to go to the region close to where the DARPA space force satellites pinpointed the invisible signature blueprint of the Nanobots. "We travel underwater in a military nuclear submarine where I can use my abilities to summon a flock or convocation of Eastern imperial eagles. As we surface at a distance from the exact location, the eagles land and can somehow place an advanced collar around their necks. If somehow, they can carry some kind of device like a smart chemical bomb, which cannot weigh more than 4 pounds. The reason why, is because the eagle's maximum carrying weight is approximately 4.4 pounds. If somehow, the advanced collar can start a low-pitched beeping when the eagles are right above their exact location. The eagles can drop the smart chemical bomb with pinpoint accuracy, there defense systems cannot detect this. The reason I chose these eagles is because they migrate to these areas naturally and won't get any unusual suspicions. You must understand, that all of this are just speculations and DARPA have their work cut out in front of them", Whit ends his assessment. Now, Tim Von Gleason, the leader of the robotic engineering scientists gives his assessments, "we will begin right away in creating advanced collars for the eagles and the smart chemical bombs that will weigh less than 4 pounds". Director Jones concludes the meeting by saying, "I would like to say at this time how proud I am to have such an amazing presence of bright minds. Especially, this incredibly coherent plan by our very own Whit, let's get to work right 24/7 and execute this plan". The team of robotic engineering scientists get started with creating the advanced collars and smart chemical bombs, they work at a 24/7 basis due to the urgency involved. In no time at all, everything is completed and ready to execute the offensive attack.

CHAPTER 29

Meanwhile, back at the messiah location Siria, the messiah's only daughter is already 12 years old celebrating her birthday. Siria, has matured quite a bit for her age, she has embraced her importance as the only heir to the messiah and fulfilling prophecy. Siria, is also striving in basic science, the messiah has placed his scientific knowledge in a series of books hidden away for her to learn his secrets in advanced science.

Chapter 30

Back at DARPA's main headquarters in Texas, Whit request that Shu comes along when the plan of attack begins. This is mainly because when they surface in the military nuclear submarine, (nuclear powered only no nuclear warheads). Shu, can use her abilities to summon any marine life to counter enemy vessels and buy them sometime to execute the plan of attack. The day finally arrives, Whit, Shu, and military personnel drive off in a military truck in the direction of the harbor. Once they arrive, everyone will board a military nuclear submarine, it's going to be a long voyage. All the amenities are put in place for such a long voyage, most of their voyage will be underwater once they pass into international waters. If you're wondering, why aren't the autonomous underwater weaponized drones aren't being used instead. When DARPA's compounds activated the emergency response systems, that automatically shut down the entire DARPA functions. After a complete diagnostic evaluation is performed and the internal cleansing of the system is complete. At that time, DARPA's entire functions will be fully operational. After a considerable amount of time, they arrive at their destination, in the Middle East there is exactly seven different oceans. The Mediterranean Sea, the Red Sea, the Dead Sea, the Black Sea, the Arabian Sea, the Caspian Sea, the Aral Sea. Due to the sensibility and classified mission the exact cannot be revealed at this time. Once, the military nuclear submarine arrives and starts to surface, everything is going as planned. DARPA space force satellites send their coordinates of the exact location of the invisible signature blueprint of the Nanobots. At the messiah location, even though, the chambers have sound proof walls and lead base protective shields. The Nanobots, invisible signature blueprints cannot be hidden, even if its invisible DARPA space force has technologies in place that can track such a substance on the earth's surface. Once, the military nuclear submarine surfaces, the hatches are opened and quickly Whit summons the flock or convocation of Eastern imperial eagles. It is extremely close to winter where these large birds of prey migrate naturally in these regions. From a distance, you can see how majestic these large prey birds truly are, once they land on the deck of the military nuclear submarine. Quickly, Whit puts the advanced collars on them, the military naval personnel come out with the smart chemical bombs. The smart chemical bombs have a small carrying harness on them, the smart chemical bombs will be activated once the eagles are at a safe distance. One by one, the flock or convocation of eagles take off with amazing grace and impressive wingspan. The eagles fly without being noticed or detection, at sea everything is calm also. Immediately, the military nuclear submarine submerges underwater, everything can be monitored from below the ocean. The flock or convocation of Eastern imperial eagles continue their flight pattern, the smart chemical bombs are activated. Once, they are above the exact location, the low frequency beeping begins. The flock or convocation of eagles release the smart chemical bombs, with Incredible accuracy the smart chemical bombs begin their fall. In only a couple of minutes the smart chemical bombs reach their mark after dropping from the sky. Be warned, the following events are extremely graphic in nature and are not suitable for everyone.

CHAPTER 31

At the time, when the smart chemical bombs were dropping from the sky, the messiah also known as (Ron Ben Ruckman), with some of his fellow scientists, and his beloved wife (Cyra), were inside the chamber underground facilities. These underground facilities aren't very deep and the only reason (Cyra) was there is because she was bringing him some tea for them to enjoy while working. As for (Siria),she is at another location just enjoying her day studying like she does many times. The minute the smart chemical bombs hit their target; the entire area explodes. The minute this explosion occurs the underground chamber is reduced to rumble. The smart chemical bombs also release a deadly chemical agent that has devastating effects. The messiah's legs are severed and his face is burned, his fellow scientists are killed instantly, his wife (Cyra) is also killed instantly. This is by far the worst day and it's not over yet, from a distance you can hear (Siria) screaming. Inside the military nuclear submarine, DARPA space force sends confirmation that the strike is a huge success. There is a low-key celebration within the crew, mostly because Ron Ben Ruckman was a part of the DARPA family. The military nuclear submarine leaves the area quickly underwater, to avoid any further confrontations. Back at the messiah's location, everybody is mobilized towards the devastating area. Everybody starts to dig out piece by piece of the rumble, this will take working crews some time to find any survivors. Siria, is being protected by armed guards and is prohibited for now to go to the site. The smart chemical bombs contain a poisonous element which contaminates the human body. These smart chemical bombs were also designed to disappear any evidence towards DARPA's involvement. The poisonous elements do not stay in the environment permanently, they are designed to insure results instantly. After a considerable time passes with crews working night and day removing the rumble. They finally make it towards the chamber underground, the dead bodies are everywhere. They remove one body after another, the crew is in total shock discovering the scientists and Cyra's dead bodies. They find the messiah barely alive, at any time he can pass away, he whispers bring my daughter. The crew tries their best to keep him alive, they tie tourniquets around both of his legs. When Siria finally arrives by her father's side, he whispers in her ear, "I will always love you and be with you, watching over you". As if destiny calls, the messiah passes away a short time after that, it seems like between the blood loss and the poison his body just couldn't take anymore suffering.

CHAPTER 32

As you can imagine, Siria yells out "No, No, no", she also sees her mom's dead body. The crews and guards take her to a safe location and tell her that both of her parents will have an ancient ceremonial burial. This event is so much for a teenage girl to bear, the suffering is overwhelming. Days after, everyone is in attendance for the ancient ceremonial funeral, Siria is in attendance. The bodies are all wrapped in white clothes from head to toe, the messiah and Cyra his wife are in a separate chamber both together in a private setting. After the words are spoken in memory of those beloved that died, after everyone tries to comfort Siria. Siria, tells the guards and everyone else that she wishes to be alone with her parents. As Siria enters the private chamber where both of her parents are covered in white clothes. They both lay on tables side by side, Siria starts to hug them both, she kneels on the ground between them. Siria, gives out a yell that is extremely loud with tears pouring down on her face, "No, No, my mom, my dad, No, No". The yells can be heard from a far distance, she continues to say "I promise you both, that whoever is responsible for this, I will be turn them into creatures. "I promise both of you that they will beg me to end their life every single day, I will not stop until I track them down". As the military nuclear submarine arrives at the harbor in Texas, as the confirmation of the success of the offensive attack reaches DARPA's main headquarters. Dircctor Jones, and everyone at DARPA don't have any idea of what they have done. Siria, will become the most wanted fugitive on planet earth and her ruthlessness shall be more feared than the legendary (Medusa, born from Greek mythology, also called Gorgo). Without knowing DARPA has created a monster with no remorse or feelings of human life.

CHAPTER 33

After a significant time passed by, the flock or convocation of Eastern imperial eagles continued their migration towards Africa. At that time, they landed inside (UNI-WORLD), where their advanced collars were removed. The eagles were also rewarded with their favorite foods and treats for a mission well done. DARPA, resumed operations as normal, all systems were diagnosed and a complete cleansing of entire systems. The robotic engineering scientists continue making breakthroughs in cracking the genetic code of the Nanobots. It will break much more time is needed, because of the revolutionary science behind this.

Chapter 34

As for Siria, she continues to grow up under extreme protection and now she is the new leader to fulfill prophecy. The origin of her name in Persian became a reality "sun-bright or glowing", many around her swear to see the flames of hell in her eyes. Siria, will continue fulfilling her father's wises in her own image, she will continue studying science. Siria, will surround herself with intelligent and loyal personnel who are extremely capable of real-life worldwide threats.